PICK AND ROLL

BY JAKE MADDOX

Text by Sean McCollum
Illustrated by Sean Tiffany

STONE ARCH BOOKS
a capstone imprint

Jake Maddox Sports Stories are published by
Stone Arch Books
a Capstone Imprint
1710 Roe Crest Drive
North Mankato, Minnesota 56003
www.mycapstone.com

Library of Congress Cataloging-in-Publication Data is available
on the Library of Congress website.

ISBN: 978-1-4965-6318-7 (library binding)
ISBN: 978-1-4965-6320-0 (paperback)
ISBN: 978-1-4965-6322-4 (eBook PDF)

Summary: Bulldogs point guard Roman is worried about his team's lack of
a center. When a towering big man nicknamed Bash shows up, Roman and
the Bulldogs are excited. But then they see that Bash's coordination hasn't
yet caught up with his body. Can Roman and Bash work out a plan to catch
the center up to speed before the season runs out?

Editor: Nate LeBoutillier
Designer: Laura Manthe
Production Specialist: Tori Abraham

Printed in Canada.
PA020

TABLE OF CONTENTS

CHAPTER 1

BIG NEWS

Roman dribbled hard to his right, stopping with a squeal of his sneakers. He pivoted back the other way. In one motion he fired a no-look bounce pass toward the basket. Viktor had faked out his man on a basket cut. He caught the pass in stride and laid it in.

Roman grinned at Mario and Rasheed, the guys they'd faked out. He blew on his fingers as if cooling them off. "Too hot for you today," he said.

The eighth-graders were playing a game of two-on-two during after-school open gym. They'd likely be four of the five starters for the Bridger Bulldogs in the upcoming season.

"You think we stand a chance this year?" Mario asked. The power forward dribbled the ball lazily between his legs as he walked up.

Roman tried for a steal. Mario simply lifted it over his head. Roman couldn't touch it there. There was no doubt Roman Carr would be the Bulldogs' point guard.

There was also no doubt he'd be the shortest guy on the team—unless he magically grew four inches overnight.

"We'll be okay," Roman said. "But I wish we had a true big man."

"Hey!" Victor said. He had played center for the last two seasons. "In case you forgot, I've got it covered. The first game isn't for two weeks yet. The Double Dog Doubleheader is three weeks away. I'll just plan on a growth spurt before that!"

"You and me both, Vik," Roman joked.

Viktor always gave everything he had on the court. But he was usually three inches shorter and twenty pounds lighter than any guy he had to guard. At least he could jump like a kangaroo.

"Hey, there's Ace," Mario said, looking over Roman's head. "One more and we can play three-on-three."

Roman turned. Ace, a Bulldogs shooting guard, was hustling toward them.

"Guys!" Ace said, gasping for air. "Do you remember that big guy we played against last year?" He paused to gulp a breath. "From Rockville, I think?" He bent over, hands on his knees.

"Sure," Roman said. "Bush, or something. Ate us alive in the low post."

"Sebastian Bosch," Viktor chimed in.

"That's it," Roman said. "Hey, wasn't he the one who pushed you all over the court, Vik?"

Viktor glared at Roman. "Nope," he said loudly. "I'm pretty sure nobody like that even exists."

Mario stepped forward. "I remember him. I went to the same basketball camp that he did a couple years ago. Everybody calls him Bash. He can bring it."

"Well, guess who I just saw upstairs," Ace said. "It's that Bash guy. And he's looking bigger than ever."

"Wait a minute," said Roman. "I think I saw him in the hallway at school. Vik, you were with me, right? I think we were outside Mrs. Jones' classroom."

"That's right," said Viktor. "There was a big kid wearing a floppy black T-shirt over baggy blue jeans. Worn out shoes. A head of messy blond hair."

"Did that head of messy blond hair tower over everyone else?" asked Ace.

"Yep," said Viktor. "Must have been about six-foot-four off the ground."

"Guys," said Roman, "we might have ourselves a new center. Now who wants to go talk to him?"

CHAPTER 2

PRACTICE

The Bulldogs trotted into the gym for their first practice. Roman loved the echo of bouncing basketballs in a gym. To him, it was the happiest sound in the world.

Roman stretched and began to warm up. He kept one eye on the door. Though the guys had convinced Bash to attend the team's sign-up meeting in school, no one had seen him around since then.

Vik proposed that maybe he'd moved back to Rockville. Still, Roman was hoping Bash would somehow show up.

"Guess he's not coming," said Ace, pulling on his kneepads. "The idea of getting a real big man was too good to be true."

"Guess you're stuck with me at center," Viktor said softly.

Roman rolled his eyes at Vik's moping. The Bulldogs formed lay-up lines. They began to get into a rhythm. Someone motioned toward the far end of the court.

"There he is!" Mario said.

Over by the gym doors stood Sebastian Bosch. He wore an old pair of sweats. He was looking nervous.

Coach Teller walked over to him. "Glad you made it, Sebastian," he said. He put an arm around the big guy's shoulders and walked him over to the team.

The guys took turns reintroducing themselves and trading high-fives.

"Let's get you some practice gear," said Coach Teller. "Follow me."

Bash put his head down and followed the coach. As Bash walked away, Roman noticed the big guy's sneakers. They were ancient. At one time, they might have been white. But they looked like they'd stepped in every mud puddle between Rockville and Bridger.

The Bulldogs continued to warm up. Bash and Coach Teller finally reappeared. Bash wore a practice jersey and shorts to go with his dirty old shoes.

Coach Teller blasted on his whistle and ran the team through defensive drills. He explained that footwork was the key to great defense. He went into great detail about how to simply stand on defense.

"Feet shoulder-width apart," he said. "Neither foot ahead of the other. Knees bent."

Coach Teller was a math teacher and cared about the smallest of details.

Next came passing and dribbling. Coach Teller emphasized using both hands equally and changing directions smoothly. Roman gave his all in every drill.

All the while, Roman kept track of his new teammate. Bash might as well have been wearing oven mitts for how well he handled passes. He couldn't dribble without staring at the ball. On defense, Bash's big feet got so tangled that it seemed like he was wearing swim fins. Roman's hopes of having a star center were draining away.

The worst moment came at the end of practice. The team lined up on one baseline. With a blast from Coach Teller's whistle, the players started sprints. After they reached half court the first time, Roman saw that Bash could only trudge. He was either in awful shape or uncoordinated. Maybe both.

Bash, his face flushed pink, finished the first set nearly a minute after everyone else. Then he stumbled over to a tall gray garbage bin, leaned over, and threw up.

The practices that week and the next all followed a similar pattern. At times, Bash showed flashes of ability. If he got his big body in position for a rebound, no one else had a chance. And he had a sweet shooting touch down low.

But mostly he was slow and clumsy. He had maybe a ten-inch vertical leap. And every practice ended with him losing his lunch in the garbage can.

Viktor started calling Bash "Barf" behind his back, and a couple guys snickered about it. Roman wondered what had happened to the guy who had played them so tough the year before.

CHAPTER 3

SEASON OPENER

At the end of two weeks' practice, the Bulldogs played the season opener against the New London Knights. It was an away game, and the Bulldogs sported their blue road uniforms.

As his team came into the gym, Roman immediately spotted his dad and sister, Julia, who was a senior. Roman raised a fist, and Julia gave him a thumbs-up. Even with her busy dance schedule, she rarely missed one of Roman's games. Likewise, Roman rarely missed her performances.

The Bulldogs formed a team circle on the sideline. Bash leaned in over Roman to put his hand in.

"Play strong, fast, and fair," Coach Teller said. "Bulldogs on three. One, two, three . . ."

"Bulldogs!" the team shouted.

Viktor started at center. He was maybe five-foot-ten and skinny as a school locker. But he was the one guy on the team who could touch the rim. Viktor skied on the opening tip-off. Roman grabbed Viktor's tap and took control.

Roman drove to the center of the free throw line, and both Knights guards came to him. Roman recognized that the white-suited Knights were in a two-three zone. Roman put a bounce pass into Ace's hands on the right wing. The shooting guard sank a fifteen-foot jumper to open the scoring.

The Knights took possession and brought the ball up the court. Rasheed jumped a passing lane and made a steal.

He launched a long lead pass. Roman caught the ball and flew in for the lay-up. It was a great start to the season. At the end of the first quarter, the Bulldogs were up, 12–7.

In the second quarter, Roman attacked at every chance. The Knights struggled to keep pace. When the halftime buzzer sounded, the Bulldogs were up 25–15. Roman came to the sideline pumping his fist.

Bash met him with a towel. "Way to roll, Roman," he said.

Bash's voice sounded squeaky. Roman could tell the big guy was relieved to be on the bench.

Things changed in the second half. The Knights knew they couldn't run with the Bulldogs, so they tried to outmuscle them. They began crashing the boards and threw the ball inside to get shots from close up.

The strategy paid off. The Bulldogs had trouble with the Knights big guys using their hips and shoulders to push the smaller players aside.

With the Knights pounding the paint, the game slowed. The Bulldogs got impatient on offense. Suddenly they couldn't rebound any of their own missed shots.

On defense, the Bulldogs watched the Knights grab offensive rebounds in bunches. The Knights front line scored several easy put-back baskets and cut the lead to four. Coach Teller told Roman to call a time-out.

"Bash, you're in for Viktor," Coach Teller said. "Concentrate on blocking out. Make them go through you for the rebound."

Bash looked more nervous than a kindergartner on the first day of school.

"Play big, Bash," Roman told him.

The Bulldogs tried to seal off the Knights posts. Sometimes they got to the rebound first. Often they didn't. The Knights center used his quickness to get an inside position on Bash.

"Come on, Barf!" Viktor barked.

"Use your size!" Roman shouted at Bash.

Roman saw Bash hang his head and then shake it. Roman felt that something bad was about to happen. It was like when he sensed a defender sneaking up for a steal.

When Ace missed his next shot, Bash did his own board-crashing. He went over the back of the Knights center and flattened him.

As the ref blew his whistle for the foul, Bash accidentally caught a Knights forward with an elbow. The Knight dropped to the floor clutching his head.

To make things worse, Bash picked up the ball and passed it hard to the ref. The ref added a technical foul. Coach Teller yanked Bash and put in Viktor.

Vik sneered as he passed Bash. "Bash, SMASH!" he said.

The Knights sank all the free throws and took the lead for good. The Bulldogs lost, 45–39. Many of the Bulldogs players were fuming in the locker room and on their way out to the bus.

On the bus, Viktor sat in front of Bash. "Way to throw away the game," he said.

"Hey, at least you didn't throw up on anyone," Roman added. Immediately, he wished he could take it back.

Bash spent the entire bus ride home with his head in his hands.

CHAPTER 4

WATCH AND LEARN

The next morning, Roman walked with
Julia to the Bridger Rec Center. Saturday
mornings, Julia taught an African Dance
class there, and Roman went to the gym.

As Roman practiced his free throws and
left-handed lay-ups, he couldn't get the
game or Bash out of his mind. After an hour,
Roman finally gave up. He stuffed his ball
into his backpack and headed for the dance
studio. When he got there, he stood in the
back and followed the steps as best he could.

Roman watched his big sister dance. She
had a gift for it. Her black braids with yellow
beads swung over her shoulders as she lost
herself in the music.

When the class ended, the students filed out, sweaty and smiling. Roman grabbed the big dust mop from the corner and began pushing it from end to end.

"You've been quiet all morning," Julia called, putting on her sneakers. "What's up?" Her voice echoed off the hardwood floor and mirrored walls.

"You saw the game yesterday," Roman said. "You saw what happened with Bash. I want to help him but don't know how to handle it. And I dissed him after the game."

Julia hopped up. "Wanna know what I saw, Pip? I saw Bash carrying something heavy, and I'm not talking about the basketball."

"I hate it when you call me Pip," Roman grumbled. "I won't be a pipsqueak forever, you know."

"Sorry . . . Pip," she cracked. She was still five inches taller than Roman.

Roman pointed at her as he made a turn with the mop. "If you're going to tease me, you better be dishing out some good advice."

"OK, then," said Julia. "Here's good advice from Big Sis. Are you listening?"

"I'm all ears," said Roman. He put the mop back in its corner.

"First," said Julia, "pay Bash a visit and clear the air. Second, I want you to bring him here tomorrow. Third, add the pick and roll to your playlist."

Roman smirked. "Pick and roll? What do you know about that?"

Julia moved a chair into the center of the dance studio. "OK," she said, "grab your ball. This chair here is guarding you."

Roman picked up his ball, shook his head, and laughed. "This should be good," he said.

"Hey, I played hoops for five years, in case you forgot," said Julia.

Roman cocked his head. "You know, I still don't know why you quit."

"Hoops or dance," said Julia. "Last year I had to make a choice. Now get ready."

Roman laughed. "Come on," he said. "I already know the pick and roll."

"Huh," said Julia. "That's funny. Did you run it with Bash last game?"

"Well," said Roman, "no."

Julia positioned herself next to the chair. "Then watch and learn," she said.

CHAPTER 5

CHECKING IN

Roman punched the doorbell and heard the ding-dong inside. His online search had found only one Bosch family in Bridger.

A tall white-haired woman opened the door. "Yes?" she asked.

"Hi, um, you must be Sebastian's . . . mom?" said Roman.

"Grandma," she replied.

"Oh," Roman said. "I'm Roman. Is Bash— uh, I mean, Sebastian—home?"

She smiled and turned. "Sebastian!" she called. She opened the door for Roman. "I'm glad he's making friends," she said. "This move hasn't been easy for him."

Bash came down the stairs of the little house. He had to duck to avoid banging his head on an overhang. His scowl was only matched by his glare at Roman.

"Let me get you boys some juice," Bash's grandma said.

"What do you want?" Bash snapped after she left the room.

"To say I'm really sorry that I made that comment on the bus yesterday," Roman said.

The two stood in silence for a long minute. Finally, Bash's grandma returned with two plastic glasses of something red. Roman thanked her. When she left, Bash led Roman out to the front porch.

Roman took a drink before speaking. "Look, we all had a rough game," he finally said. "It wasn't just you."

"It's over," Bash said. "I'm done."

"What?" said Roman. "No way. You stunk it up yesterday, but I can see it's coming back to you in practice."

Bash turned and headed for the door.

Roman winced at his own words. "Dude! I'm sorry! You didn't stink. That's not what I meant. Or maybe it is, but we're gonna be a better team with you than without you. That's what I know. We could use you."

Bash spun and stormed back. He was a foot taller than Roman and loomed over him. Roman had to lean back to look Bash in the eyes.

"You could use me, huh?" said Bash. "Great. Use me, then. Use it all up." He spat over the railing.

Roman thought of what Julia had said. She was sure that something bigger was going on with Bash.

"Hey," Roman said, "take it easy. Is there something else going on?"

"Ever jump schools in the middle of the year, Roman?" said Bash. "Ever have to leave your friends? Leave your family?"

Roman shook his head. "Why'd you have to leave Rockville?" he asked.

"Because life stinks," said Bash. "Because the warehouse where my mom and dad worked closed down. Because shipping me here means one less fat mouth to feed."

Roman didn't know what to say. That is, until he did. "Hey, Bash," he said. "Let's go shoot some hoops."

CHAPTER 6

PICKING AND ROLLING

Carrying his scarred basketball under his left arm, Roman walked up to the courts at the city park. Bash walked next to him. Roman liked the city park courts. The rims were always level, never bent. He lofted a fifteen-footer.

Swish.

Bash took a shot. It hit the heel of the rim and ricocheted with a loud, metallic *bong.* Roman caught it on the fly and then looped a pass back to Bash. Bash caught it with one big hand and sank an easy finger roll.

"That's the touch I'm talking about," said Roman. He hesitated. "Hey, can I show you something? Ever hear of the pick and roll?"

Bash half-nodded and half-shrugged.

Roman dragged a trash can onto the court and set it at the top of the key. "Imagine we're at practice. This trash can is Viktor, and he is guarding me. You come out and set a hard pick on him."

"Love to," Bash said.

Roman laughed. "But you can't run him over!" he said.

Bash couldn't block a smile. He shuffled out and stood next to the can.

Roman dribbled right, brushing past Bash. "Now as I scrape by, you do a reverse pivot," he said. "Then you roll toward the basket."

Bash spun the wrong way and stumbled.

"Try again," said Roman. He gracefully demonstrated the move in the same way that Julia had shown him.

The boys repeated the play. This time Bash pivoted the right way. He made a nice roll, and Roman put the ball in the big guy's palms.

Bash kissed the shot off the weathered backboard, and the ball settled into the net.

They ran the play ten more times—five going to the left, five to the right. Bash set the imaginary pick, Roman dribbled past him. Bash then rolled toward the basket, and Roman got him the ball.

"The key is for me to scrape by, and for you to pivot and keep my man on your back," Roman said. Bash was getting the hang of it faster than Roman thought he would.

"Seems pretty easy with no one on D," Bash said.

"But it's tough to defend when you—when *we*, I mean—do it right," Roman replied. "The pros use it all the time. But I've got to be hitting my shots if they double-team you."

Roman pulled up and sank a jumper from the right side of the free throw circle. What Roman lacked in size he'd learned to make up for with a quick release.

They ran the play again and again.

After multiple smooth passes and made baskets, Roman wondered if it was the right time to risk an embarrassing question.

"So . . . Bash," he said. "How do you feel about dance lessons?"

CHAPTER 7

BASKETBALL BOOGIE

Roman and Bash sat outside the rec center dance studio. The final notes of a song faded behind the door. A minute later the door opened. Bouncing and laughing, a group of young dancers filed out.

"I don't know about this," Bash said.

"No worries, Bash," Roman told him. "You'll dig my sister. She's somehow kind of intense and very chill at the same time."

On cue, Julia's head peeked out of the door. "Hey, Pip," she said to Roman.

Roman rolled his eyes and smiled.

Julia turned to Bash. "You must be Bash," she said. "Great to meet you! Come in."

The teammates got up and followed her in.

"I saw the game last Friday, and you guys are going to be fine," she started. "But you've got a couple things to work on."

Roman wasn't super interested in a pep talk. Bash, though, studied Julia closely and seemed to be listening to every word. Roman decided not to complain.

"First," said Julia, "you win as a team, you lose as a team." Her eyes locked on Roman. "Sooner or later it'll be you who comes up short and needs a teammate to pick you up."

Roman felt his face get warm.

"Second," said Julia, "your moves are only as good as your footwork. You guys are rusty. Since there's nothing that teaches footwork like dancing, I'm here to teach you a move or two."

Julia turned so she was facing the same way as Roman and Bash. She pointed a small remote at her laptop. A twangy guitar and fiddle started up.

"Are you serious?" Roman said to his sister.

A lonesome-sounding singer belted out some cheesy lyrics.

"Is this," said Bash, "country music?"

Julia laughed. "This is line dancing! It's one of the simplest ways to learn how to dance."

Bash shot Roman a worried look. Roman raised his eyebrows and shrugged.

Julia counted off. She began a series of steps. "Grapevine to the right. Side-step, cross. Side-step, feet together, clap. Now back to the left."

Though their feet were in knots at first, the boys started to catch on. Roman began to feel relief that the song was slow enough for them to keep up.

"Hey," Bash called out. "This is just the Electric Boogie!"

"Indeed it is, Bash," Julia said over her shoulder. "It's the Basketball Boogie!"

Roman watched Bash out of the corner of his eye. The big guy was getting into it. His shoulders relaxed as he dipped his hips. When Bash put some flair into the hand claps, Roman yipped liked a coyote.

They learned two more dances, each a little faster. They pivoted on their toes, leaned in, leaned back, and spun again.

Julia stopped her own dancing to watch them. "That's it," she said. "Stay light on your feet. Anticipate the next step."

When they finished the last song, Julia applauded them. "Good dancing, guys," she said. "Now let's dance the pick and roll." She fetched a basketball from behind a speaker.

With hip-hop playing in the background, Julia walked them through the pick and roll. Like with the line dancing, Bash started out doubtfully, resisting Julia's instructions.

Within minutes, though, she had won him over. She showed them different ways defenders guard him and how to react.

When she thought they'd had enough, Julia said, "Well?"

Bash didn't say anything, but he grinned. It was a real smile.

The smile shocked Roman. It dawned on Roman that it was probably the first time he'd seen Bash let down his guard.

CHAPTER 8

THE DOUBLE DOG

The Double Dog Doubleheader was a yearly tradition between the Bridger Bulldogs and Hudson Huskies.

Each year, the neighboring towns of Bridger and Hudson played a home-and-home Saturday doubleheader of basketball. The first game was in the morning. The second was in the evening. The two towns, which were ten miles apart, would each get to host one game.

Whichever team won the first game got the Dog Bone trophy. The winner of the second game won the Dog House trophy. Both trophies had engravings of the results of years gone by. To be able to win both trophies and keep them in the school's trophy case for an entire year was a special honor.

Fans got into it. Some even came dressed up in dog-themed costumes. One year, they supposedly let actual dogs in. It did not go well. Dogs were no longer allowed in the gym.

This year Rasheed had designed a funny video to promote the games. It showed a fierce-looking bulldog carrying a bone. Rasheed had looped the scene so the dog looked like it was dancing. The video got hundreds of hits on the school website.

In the Hudson Middle School visiting locker room, Roman double-knotted his laces. The Bulldogs were about to warm up, but Bash was missing. He hadn't made the bus.

"You talked to Bash yesterday, right?" Roman asked Mario.

Mario shrugged. "Yesterday everything was cool. He was spending the night with his folks in Rockville, I guess."

"Isn't that an hour away?" Roman said.

Mario nodded.

Roman slammed his locker door. He had been feeling new confidence in the team. The most recent practices had been the Bulldogs' best ones yet. They were playing faster and looser.

Better yet, Bash seemed to be finding his groove since the dance lesson. He was mastering the pick and roll. Plus he was getting his stamina back—no more barfing.

Coach Teller passed by, mumbling. He checked his phone and then dropped it back into the pocket of his rumpled sport coat.

"You hear from Bash?" Roman said.

"Nope," said Coach Teller. After a moment he clapped his hands together and said, "Let's dance with who we got, Bulldogs!"

He didn't get much of a response.

"Woof! Woof!" barked Coach Teller. "Come on! Who's ready for the Double Dog?"

A few of the guys started giggling and barking back. Mario did a dance move that somehow looked like the bulldog in Rasheed's video. Guys cracked up. It seemed to help lighten the mood.

During warm-ups, Roman recognized some Huskies players who attended the same sports camps as him. The center was a tall redhead named Roddy. He was a beanpole, but he could really run, jump, and shoot.

The Huskies wore their white uniforms with dark blue numbers. The Bulldogs dressed in their blue road unis. Roddy easily outjumped Viktor for the opening tip and scored with a half hook. On defense, the Huskies fell back into man-to-man.

The Bulldogs' first possessions did not go well. Several blocked shots by Roddy proved the lane was closed. Nobody on the Bulldogs starting front line—Viktor, Mario, or Rasheed—could get anything going near the basket.

Meanwhile, Ace and Roman tossed up mostly bricks from the outside.

The Huskies had built a 30–15 lead by halftime. "I think they shrunk the rim," Ace griped in the locker room. "We could really have used Bash."

"Tell me about it," Roman replied.

Viktor slumped over, staring at the floor. Roman realized that he might have, again, said the wrong thing.

In the second half, Roman tried to get the Bulldogs back in the game by pushing the pace.

Whenever the Bulldogs tried to fast break, though, the Huskies were quick to get back on defense. Even when they didn't, Roddy often chased down plays from behind.

All the Bulldogs starters were on the bench as the clock wound down. Game one had been a blowout—Huskies 52, Bulldogs 31.

Roman chewed on a white towel. It tasted like bleach. His face burned as he watched the Huskies hoist the Dog Bone trophy.

Mario stuck an elbow in Roman's ribs. "Hey, look," he said. "There's Bash."

Bash was with his family by the lobby doors. Roman recognized Bash's grandma. Next to her were two other adults who must have been his parents. One of them held a young girl.

"Lot of good it does us now," Viktor said.

Bash hurried over to his teammates as the final buzzer sounded. "Sorry guys," he said. "We got a flat tire. And then I thought the first game was at Bridger, so we went—"

"Oh, *that's* what happened," Viktor shouted, interrupting Bash. "We were worried maybe you got carsick!"

Roman was in his teammate's face before the last word was out of Viktor's mouth. "Shut it, Vik," he said. "We win as a team. We lose as a team."

"Well, our team just got smoked!" said Viktor. "So maybe Bash should feel as embarrassed as the rest of us."

No one said anything for a long moment until Bash spoke up.

"Sorry I missed the game," Bash said quietly. "But I'm here now."

CHAPTER 9

DOUBLE DOG REMATCH

That evening, the Bulldogs came out of the locker room in their home whites. A fan in a rubber Bulldog mask approached Roman and Bash. "How'd it go?" a muffled girl's voice said. The fan raised the mask. It was Julia. Roman explained the disaster of game one.

Julia shook her head but smiled. She gave Bash a playful swat on the shoulder. "You gotta show up, big guy!" she remarked.

Bash nodded and blushed.

"Run that pick and roll," she continued. "They won't be expecting big changes. But you, Bash, are a *big* change."

"Except Coach will probably keep me on the bench for being gone earlier," Bash said.

"He'll put you in," Julia said. "They need you. Just be ready when your number's called." She shooed them onto the court for warm-ups.

The teams met at midcourt for the tip-off.

"Sad we've got to do this again," said Roddy, the Huskies center, to Roman. "We're going to try to double your score. I'm thinking sixty-thirty. Sound about right?"

"We'll see," Roman said.

The evening game started out the same as the morning one. Viktor did his best to keep Roddy from backing toward the basket. Still, the Huskies big man sank a short turnaround jumper on Hudson's first possession.

Ace missed the Bulldogs' first shot. Roddy rebounded, and the Huskies raced up the court. Their point guard made the lay-up and was fouled. After a free throw, it was 5–0.

On offense, Roman called out plays. He motioned for Viktor to clear the lane. Roddy stayed near the basket, guarding the paint like a spider waiting for flies. Roman set Viktor up with a clean look, but Viktor missed. Then Viktor missed another couple open shots.

The score was 9–2 near the end of the first quarter before Coach Teller replaced Viktor with Bash. Bringing the ball up the court, Roman was glad to see Hudson had stayed in its man-to-man defense.

Roman dribbled to his right. He swirled his index finger in the air, the signal for the pick and roll. Bash picked, and Roman scraped by.

Roddy called out, "Switch!" Now he was defending Roman. But that left the Hudson guard on Bash—the mismatch Roman wanted. Bash executed a perfect reverse pivot, leaving the Huskies guard to defend Bash.

Roman sent a bounce pass between Roddy's long legs. Bash nabbed it and banged home the basket.

"That's my steal next time, squirt," Roddy said to Roman on the way down the floor.

On their next possession, the Huskies realized they were in for a real fight. Roddy tried to lean into Bash, but Bash was too big to move. Roddy caught the entry pass about ten feet from the basket.

Rasheed swept in from Roddy's blind side and made a clean steal. The Bulldogs exploded into a three-on-one fast break for an easy bucket. Another steal by Mario, another break, and suddenly the Bulldogs had closed within one point.

The score at the end of one quarter was Bridger 12, Hudson 11. The Huskies weren't laughing now, Roman noticed.

All the Bulldogs players saw that they could hang with these guys. They had their arms around each other's shoulders as Coach Teller led the huddle. Bulldog fans were woofing in the stands.

The second quarter started with a similar script. Roddy got twitchy scanning for the double-team. He usually passed the ball instead of trying to shoot. That led to Huskies turnovers and rushed jumpers. Some went in, but most didn't.

On defense, Hudson switched to a 2–3 zone. The shift made the pick and roll tougher to run. Still, Bash's presence inside opened Ace, Rasheed, and Roman for outside shots. The fast break was rolling too.

There was about a minute to go in the first half when Roddy decided to try some trickery.

He backed in on Bash but suddenly stumbled forward, making it look as if Bash had given him a shove. The ref immediately called the foul on Bash.

"I didn't touch him," Bash told Roman.

The teams lined up for free throws. Roddy sank two.

On the Huskies' next offensive possession, Roddy repeated the act. He backed in with his dribble, but then flopped forward. Again the ref called the foul on Bash, his third.

"What?" Bash shouted. The ref gave him a warning look.

This time Roddy made the first free throw and missed the second. A Huskies forward got the offensive rebound and put it in. The score was knotted at 26 at halftime.

CHAPTER 10

FINISHING STRONG

Bash started the third quarter on the bench.

"Can't afford for you to get that fourth foul," Coach Teller said. "Five fouls and you're out."

"Big surprise," Roman heard Viktor say.

Roman warned Vik by shaking his head.

With Bash out, Hudson went back to its original game plan on defense—man-to-man. They fed Roddy the ball on offense. Viktor did his best, but he didn't have the size to guard the Huskies center.

The Bulldogs tried double-teaming Roddy, but the Huskies had made their own adjustment. They rotated their best shooters to where Roddy could pass out to them. Hudson quickly reclaimed the lead.

Roman countered with ball-handling skills. He sliced into the lane. When the Huskies collapsed on him, he looked for the white jersey of the open man. Ace hit a 3-pointer. Viktor and Mario sank mid-range jumpers.

Without Bash in the middle, though, Roddy was back to sweeping the boards clean. There were no second shots to be had for the Bulldogs when they missed.

Roman pulled out every trick he knew. On one breakaway, he could feel a Hudson forward closing in from behind. Instead of going for a lay-up, Roman bounced a high pass off the glass. Just as Roman had hoped, Rasheed was trailing at full speed. He caught the ball and scored in one smooth motion.

Still, the Huskies led 40–34 after three periods.

"Bash, you're in," Coach Teller said during the break. "We've got to slow the center. Front him." Coach demonstrated what he meant.

The change confused Roddy and the Huskies. Bash now parked his bigness in front of the tall redhead, not behind. Bash picked off one pass easily and started a fast break that ended in two points.

The Huskies again tried to get the ball to their center. This time a lob pass sailed over Roddy's outstretched arm and out of bounds.

Still, Hudson kept trying to force the ball to their big man. On one play, Roddy got the ball and faked. Bash flattened him going for the block. The ref whistled Bash for the foul, and Roddy waggled four fingers at Bash.

Roman got in front of Bash. "Careful now," he said.

Roddy cashed in his free throws. On offense, Roman noticed the Huskies had gone back to a zone to take away the pick and roll. Roman responded by working the ball around the perimeter. When the Huskies got out of position, Roman drove the lane.

Roddy was waiting there. When Roddy covered Roman, Roman passed to Mario slashing along the baseline. Mario laid it in.

The teams went back and forth until Roman hit a step-back jumper to cut the Huskies lead to two. One minute remained.

The Huskies attempted to stall but threw away a pass. The Bulldogs wasted no time on offense, and Rasheed was fouled on a drive. He fell hard. He got up limping but insisted on shooting his free throws. He missed the first, sank the second, and then had to come out of the game.

Viktor replaced him. Roman went over to Viktor, and they pounded fists.

"We good?" Roman asked.

Viktor gave a cranky look but nodded.

Up by one, the Huskies guards tried to run out the clock. The Bulldogs double-teamed. Finally, the Huskies point guard succeeded in looping a pass over Bash to Roddy. The big redhead turned to bank it in. He didn't even jump, as if to rub in the easy score.

Viktor didn't let him. He flew across the lane. With a perfectly-timed jump, he swatted the shot for a clean block. Roman tracked down the ball and checked the clock. Ten seconds remained. Hudson was still up, 50–49.

Roman dashed forward, pushing the ball into the frontcourt. To his surprise, the Huskies had gone back to man-to-man defense.

Roman didn't even call a play—he just met eyes with Bash. Bash knew what to do. He lumbered toward Roman and set the pick.

But Roddy didn't pop out to guard Roman. He stayed with Bash to cover the roll. That left Roman an opening into the lane. Roman drove hard and pulled up for a short shot.

Viktor's man was waiting for just that. He closed on Roman quickly. In mid-air, Roman realized he'd never get the shot over the guy. He curved his body and somehow got the pass to Viktor in the corner. Viktor went up for the shot. But now Roddy was flying at him.

Aw, no! Roman thought as he watched the ball's arc. It was coming up way short. Then Roman realized it wasn't a shot, but a pass. Bash caught it near the basket. He banked it in just as the buzzer sounded.

The crowd erupted. The Bulldogs bench spilled onto the court in celebration.

"BASH!" Roman and Viktor both howled the big guy's name. They leapt on his wide back.

After the cheers died down, the Bulldogs accepted the Dog House trophy. The crowd clapped and laughed as the team danced the Bulldog dance around it. Afterward, Roman met Bash's family.

Bash was holding the little girl. "My sister Megan," he told Roman.

Roman bumped fists with her.

Bash grinned. "Mom and Dad just got offered jobs here in Bridger," he said.

"Seriously?" said Roman.

"Yep," said Bash. "You and me? Looks like we're going to be running that pick and roll for quite a while."

AUTHOR BIO

Sean McCollum grew up hoping to play guard for the Milwaukee Bucks. Alas, he proved too short and too slow. He still loves hoops but traded in his hightops for a laptop and a life as a wandering writer. He has written some fifty books for kids, tweens, and teens. You can find out more about Sean's work at his website—www.kidfreelance.com.

ILLUSTRATOR BIO

Sean Tiffany has worked in the illustration and comic book field for more than twenty years. He has illustrated more than sixty children's books for Capstone and has been an instructor at the famed Joe Kubert School in northern New Jersey. Raised on a small island off the coast of Maine, Sean now resides in Boulder, Colorado, with his wife, Monika, their son, James, a cactus named Jim, and a room full of entirely too many guitars.

GLOSSARY

assist (uh-SIST)—a pass that leads to a score

fundamentals (fuhn-duh-MEN-tuhls)—basic skills such as dribbling, passing, and shooting

low post (LOH POHST)—a position or place near the basket, typically on either side of the free throw lane

pick (PIK)—a play in which an offensive player stands against a teammate's defender in order to block that defender

pick and roll (PIK AND ROHL)—a play in which a player sets a pick for a teammate with the ball and then cuts or "rolls" to the basket

pivot (PIV-uht)—a point on which something turns or balances

possession (puh-ZESH-uhn)—refers to the time that the offensive team has the ball

ricochet (RIK-uh-shay)—to hit a hard surface and go in a different direction

rotate (ROH-tate)—to spin around

stamina (STAM-uh-nuh)—the energy and strength to keep doing something for a long time

tradition (truh-DISH-uhn)—a custom, idea, or belief passed through time

DISCUSSION QUESTIONS

1. Bash's size seems to make him an ideal center, but he has some issues. What are they, and how do they hold him back?

2. Can you find examples of Roman being a good teammate? A bad teammate? Explain.

3. The Double Dog Doubleheader is a fun tradition. What traditions does your team, school, or town have?

WRITING PROMPTS

1. Imagine that Roman and Bash enter a dance contest. Write the scene using details.

2. At the end of the Double Dog Doubleheader, Bash makes the winning shot. Imagine a different result and write it.

3. Bash and Roman perfect the pick-and-roll play. Is there a certain play you're good at? Write a description of it.

MORE ABOUT...THE PICK AND ROLL

The pick and roll is a big part of every NBA offense. In the 2015–16 season, teams ran it on almost 25 percent of their half-court possessions.

Big men don't always roll to the basket after setting a pick. If they're good outside shooters, they might "pick and pop" for an open jumper. The pick and pop is one of the signature moves of Dirk Nowitzki of the Dallas Mavericks.

The NBA counts "screen assists." This statistic tallies great picks that result in scores. In 2016–17, Marcin Gortat of the Washington Wizards led the league with 6.2 screen assists per game.

Karl Malone and John Stockton are considered the best pick-and-roll team in NBA history. The Utah Jazz duo played together from 1985–2003.